NIKI L   . Design.
He came to England in 1970 under contract to CBS to write and record songs,
then started work as a graphic designer, illustrator and design teacher.
In 1978 his first book, *The Little Girl Who Lived Down the Road*, won him a
British Arts Council Illustration Award. Since 1980 he has lived in South Africa
teaching, illustrating, composing and recording.
Not So Fast Songololo won him a Parent's Choice Award in the US
and was made into a Weston Woods videotape.
In 1995 he won an IBBY Honours Award for *All the Magic in the World*.
In the same year, *Why the Sun and Moon Live in the Sky* was chosen by the *New York
Times Literary Supplement* as one of their ten best illustrated books, and a year
later it was awarded the Anne Izard Story Teller's Choice Award.
Bravo Zan Angelo! was his first book for Frances Lincoln.
It was followed by *Jamela's Dress*, Nola Turkington's *The Dancer, Fly, Eagle, Fly!*
with Christopher Gregorowski and *What's Cooking Jamela?*
Niki Daly lives in Mowbray, Cape Town with
his wife the illustrator Jude Daly, and their two sons.

For my friend Miriam Makalima

Not so Fast Songololo copyright © Frances Lincoln Limited 2001
Text and illustrations copyright © Niki Daly 1985, 2001

First published in Great Britain in 1985
by Victor Gollancz Ltd.

This edition first published in 2001 by Frances Lincoln Limited,
4 Torriano Mews, Torriano Avenue, London, NW5 2RZ.

First paperback edition 2001

British Library Cataloguing in Publication Data available on request

0-7112-1765-3 paperback

Printed in Singapore

5 7 9 8 6 4

Not so Fast
SONGOLOLO

● Story & Pictures by **Niki Daly** ●

Listen to the noise!

"Weh, weh, weh!" Uzuti is crying.

Adelaide is shouting. "Mongi, give me back my
yellow pen!"

Mama calls, "Shepherd, get up! Come on, Shepherd."

Mr Motiki's dog is barking at someone coming up the road.

Shepherd likes doing things slowly.

He sings a little, then he pulls on his T-shirt.

He plays a little and then he puts on his shoes – his tackies.

They are very old tackies.

When they were new they belonged to Mongi.

But now they have holes in them
and they belong to Shepherd.

Mr Motiki's dog is still barking at someone
coming up the road.
Only an old person walks so slowly.
Look how she walks a little
and then stops to lean on her stick for a while.
Mr Motiki's dog has stopped barking.
Instead he is wagging his tail.
It's OK. It's only Gogo, Shepherd's old granny.

Gogo is old, but her face shines like new shoes.

Her hands are large and used to hard work,

but when they touch, they are gentle.

   She rests her hands on Shepherd's shoulders and says,

"I need someone to help me today."

Shepherd keeps quiet and listens carefully.

   "I must do my shopping in the city.

Yu! Those mad cars! And the traffic lights!

That little Green Man mixes me up," says Gogo.

   Mama says, "OK, Shepherd will go with you.

He is a big boy now."

Shepherd likes doing things slowly.
So he walks a little, and then he stops
to kick an old beer can. Twang!
The can dances down the street.
Gogo walks slowly behind.
 "Haai," sighs Gogo.
She is out of breath when they reach
the bus stop. The beer can lies still in
the hot street. When the bus comes,
it squashes the can flat.
This makes Shepherd laugh.

"Stop laughing and help me on to the bus," scolds Gogo. Shepherd doesn't know what he should do – push or pull his old Gogo. Gogo sees the worried look on his face and laughs.

"Here, hold my stick. I'm too old to kick a can down the street. But I can still climb on to a bus!"

The bus is full.

Standing room only.

Shepherd stands close to Gogo.

She is wearing her best dress.

He counts the colours in the pattern.

Red, green, pink, black,

blue, yellow and orange.

The bus stops and some people climb out.

Now Shepherd and Gogo can sit down

next to a window.

"Look," says Gogo, "look at all those mad cars!"
Shepherd knows all about cars.
He can tell Gogo the names of all the cars.
   "Volkswagen...Morris...Ford..."
Gogo thinks he is very clever as he plays his car game
all the way to the city.

"Shu!" says Gogo. "So many people!"
Everyone walks so quickly.
Shepherd walks ahead of Gogo.
Then he stops and waits for her.
She looks older in the city.

Sometimes, while he is waiting for her,
Shepherd looks at all the things
in the big shop windows.
Here is a toyshop. Look! A toy Volkswagen!

Here is a shoe shop. See, tackies!
Shepherd looks down at his old tackies
and then at the ones in the window.
They are bright red with stripes down the side.
   "What are you looking at?" asks Gogo.
She has caught up at last.
   "Look, Gogo," says Shepherd, "bright red tackies!"
Gogo looks at the new tackies, and then she sees
Shepherd's old tackies and she clicks her tongue.

Now they must cross the busy road to reach OK Bazaars.

"There's the little Green Man!" shouts Shepherd.
Gogo looks worried, so Shepherd takes her hand
and leads her slowly across the zebra crossing.
Just before they reach the other side
the little Green Man disappears.

"Haai!" scolds Gogo,"That little Green Man
mixes me up!"

In the big shop, Gogo looks at her shopping list.
She must buy some groceries,
a new plastic cloth, a mug,
and a bottle to keep beans in.
Everything costs so much money.
Gogo keeps her money in a little bag
which she pins to the inside of her sleeve.
There it is always safe.

Now it is time to cross that busy road again.

Hey! There's the little Green Man.

They pass the flower sellers and a clothes shop.

Look! Here's the shoe shop with those bright red tackies looking so nice and new. Shepherd presses his nose against the shop window for a last look.

"Come, Songololo!" calls Gogo.

Songololo is her special name for her grandson.

Now, see! Instead of passing by,

Gogo goes straight into the shoe shop.

She really does!

Shepherd looks at Gogo's old shoes.

They look like worn-out tyres on an old car.

"How much are those red tackies in the window?"
asks Gogo.

"Four rands," the man replies.

"Will you see if they fit the boy?" asks Gogo.

Shepherd takes off his tackies and slowly fits his feet
into the new ones. The man presses around his toes.

"They fit him very well," he says.

Shepherd feels so happy that it hurts him just to sit still.

He looks at Gogo and gives her a big smile.

"Shu!" says Gogo, as she takes out her money bag.

"One...two...three...four rands," she counts.

Gogo says that Shepherd may keep on his new tackies.

He puts his old ones into the new shoe box.

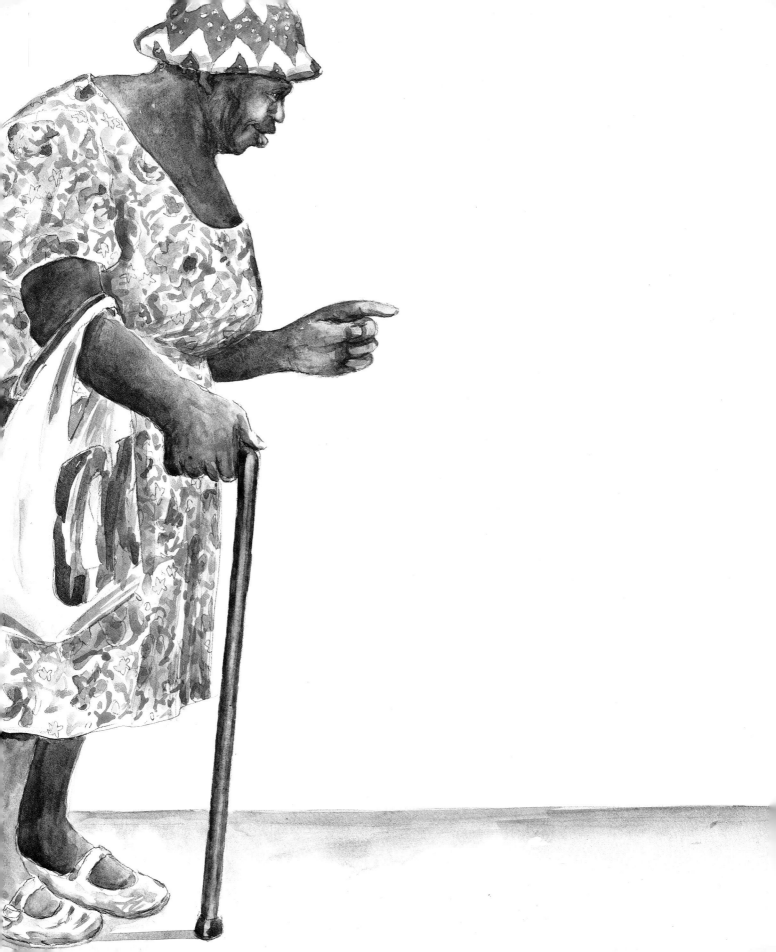

Now see how that boy can walk!
"Not so fast, Songololo!" calls out Gogo.

At the bus terminus Gogo sits down and rests.
Shepherd sits next to her with his feet on the bench
so that he can look at the new tackies.

"You know, Gogo," says Shepherd softly,
"these are very nice red tackies."

Gogo looks down at her old shoes and says,
"Yes. Maybe if I had red tackies with white stripes
I would walk as fast as you."
Shepherd looks at Gogo – and then they both laugh.